LEABHARLANNA CHONTAE FHINE GALL

FINGAL COUNTY LIBRARIES

JNF
Bot 8

Items should be returned on or before the last date shown below. Items may be renewed by personal application, writing, telephone or by accessing the online Catalogue Service on Fingal Libraries' website. To renew give date due, borrower ticket number and PIN number if using online catalogue. Fines are charged on overdue items and will include postage incurred in recovery. Damage to, or loss of items will be charged to the borrower

Date Due	Date Due	Date Due
14. JUL 05		
13. FEB 06,		
30. AUG		
12. JAN 09,		

This book belongs to

OXFORD
UNIVERSITY PRESS

Great Clarendon Street, Oxford OX2 6DP

Oxford University Press is a department of the University of Oxford.
It furthers the University's objective of excellence in research, scholarship,
and education by publishing worldwide in

Oxford New York

Athens Auckland Bangkok Bogotá Buenos Aires Calcutta
Cape Town Chennai Dar es Salaam Delhi Florence Hong Kong Istanbul
Karachi Kuala Lumpur Madrid Melbourne Mexico City Mumbai
Nairobi Paris São Paulo Singapore Taipei Tokyo Toronto Warsaw

Oxford is a registered trade mark of Oxford University Press
in the UK and in certain other countries

Text copyright © Paul May 2000
Illustrations copyright © Paul Dainton 2000

The moral rights of the author and artist have been asserted

First published 2000

Hardback ISBN 0–19–910651-7
Paperback ISBN 0–19–910652-5
Pack of 6 ISBN 0-19-910757-2
Pack of 36 ISBN 0-19-910758-0

This edition is also available in Oxford Reading Tree
Branch Library Stages 8-10 Pack A

3 5 7 9 10 8 6 4 2

Printed in Spain by Edelvives.

Contents

▶ The fastest car in the world

The sun beats down on the flat desert sand. Far away there is a black dot. Behind the dot is a cloud of dust. The rocket car is on its way.

The black dot grows bigger. It streaks across the desert like a bullet. Flames shoot from the back of the car, but where is the roar of the engines?

Dust fills the air, and then the desert shakes. The rocket car has gone. Now its sound has arrived!

BOOM!

The rocket car is travelling faster than sound. It is the fastest car in the world.

Thrust SSC

First cars

Only a hundred years ago, the world
was a quieter place. Most people in
the world had never seen a car.
The first cars were dangerous and
exciting. Sometimes they exploded!

Steam made the first cars work.
One had no brakes. It crashed!
One was very hard to steer. If you
turned the steering wheel left – the
car went right!

In England, a man walked in front
of every car. He waved a red flag.
"Get out of the way!" he cried.
"A car is coming!"

Nicholas Cugnot's
1769 Steam Fardier

Then a new kind of engine was invented. It was light and powerful. The engine burned petrol, and it was perfect for cars.

The first petrol cars were made by hand. Each car took a long time to make. Each car cost a lot of money. Only rich people could afford them.

1903 Renault petrol engine car

Model T Ford (Tin Lizzie)

Henry Ford was an American.
He loved making cars. "I will build
a factory," he said, "I will make
cheap cars." He thought of a clever
way to make cars quickly. The
cars moved through the factory,
and each worker had his own
special job. The workers fixed the
cars together.

Out of the factory came thousands
and thousands of cars! People loved
them. They called them Tin Lizzies.

Robots and computers

Car factories still work the same way. Cars move through the factory, but now robots help with the work. Robots fix the cars together! Computers tell the robots what to do. And people tell the computers what to do.

Factories today make cars very quickly.

Factories all over the world make millions and millions of cars every year.

Guess how many cars there are in the world today. Ten million? One hundred million? No.

Today there are more than five hundred million cars!

▶ Cars, cars, cars

Look out of the window. Cars are
everywhere! There are huge cars—
and there are tiny cars.

**Cadillac Stretch
Limousine**

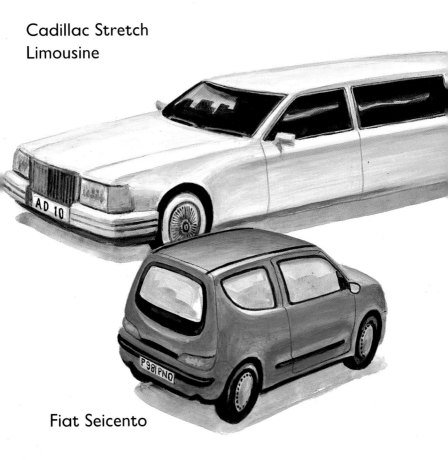

Fiat Seicento

There are new, expensive cars –

Rolls Royce
Silver Spirit

and there are old bangers.

Ford Cortina
Mark II

Fast cars zoom past – and police cars
chase them.

New York police car

Ferrari F40

Some cars can even drive through fields and rivers.

Four-wheel drive Jeep

Every car looks different – but every car works the same way.

▶ Explosions

Every car has an engine. Inside the engine, petrol mixes with air. The spark plug makes a spark, and the petrol and air explode! That's what makes a car go – explosions!

Each explosion pushes a piston down – like your legs pushing pedals on a bike.

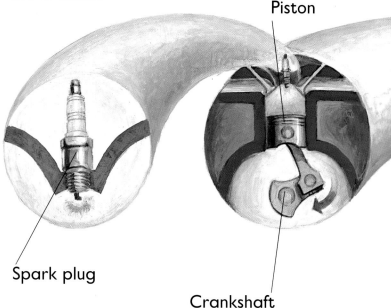

Piston

Spark plug

Crankshaft

The force of the piston turns the crankshaft. Then the crankshaft turns the gears.

The gears send the force to the wheels of the car. The car wheels turn, and the car begins to move.

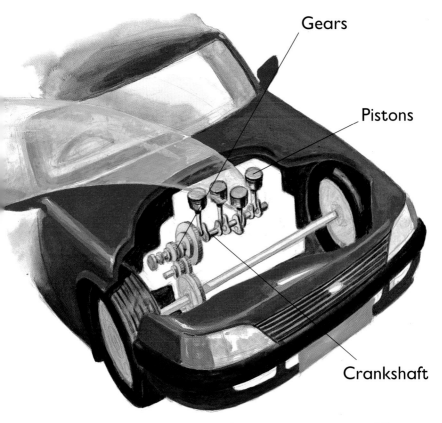

Gears

Pistons

Crankshaft

Every car has brakes. The brakes on
a car work like the brakes on a bike.
They rub against the wheels, and the
wheels slow down. But don't put
them on too hard – or you'll skid!

Every car has steering. You turn the
steering wheel, and then the front
wheels turn. But be careful how you
steer – don't go round the corners
too fast! Drive carefully – or you'll
have an accident!

▶ Danger!

The night is rainy. The road is slippery and wet. Here comes a car – it's going too fast. Another car is coming. Wheels skid. Brakes screech.
CRASH!

Metal crumples like paper. But inside the cars, airbags fill with air. Seatbelts hold the passengers. These people are lucky. They are hurt, but they are alive.

All over the world cars kill thousands of people. There's only one place to drive fast – the racetrack!

▶ No speed limit

Some people love danger! They love to go racing in cars. The racetrack is an exciting place.

Noise fills the air. Lights flash on

... 1 ... 2 ... 3 ... 4 ... 5 ...

The cars scream away from the start. They fly around the track. There is no speed limit here. One hundred miles an hour ... one hundred and fifty!

Here comes a bend.
Slow down ...
    change gear ...
        brakes ...
            steering ...

And off again, round and round the track until the chequered flag comes down.

The winners celebrate. And after the race they drive home safely – in ordinary cars.

Car trouble

It is early in the morning. People rush from their houses. They jump into their cars. They rush to work. They rush to school. They rush to the shops.

Thousands of cars rush into the city every day. If there are too many cars, the traffic cannot move. It's quicker to ride a bike!

It's no fun driving a car in a traffic
jam. It's no fun to be in the city
when the air is filled with fumes
and noise.

Did you know . . .
Cities like Athens, Mexico City and New Delhi have major problems with car pollution.

Sometimes the city air is hard to breathe. Sometimes the air turns to smog. Sometimes whole cities say, "Please! No cars today!"
On other days the fumes disappear.

You cannot see them, but they are
still there. They mix with the air.

The fumes make people ill, and they
have made the weather change.
Some people say, "Get rid of cars!"
But other people say, "We want to
keep our cars."
So what can we do?

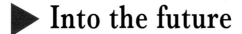 # Into the future

People are trying to invent a new
kind of car – a car that is clean
and quiet.

This car looks new and strange.
It makes its own fuel – from sunlight!
Perhaps one day every car will be
like this.

And perhaps computers will talk to cars. Computers will tell cars where to go. There will be no more traffic jams. The cities will be clean and quiet.

Or perhaps the car of the future will be stranger still. Perhaps nobody has thought of it yet.

Perhaps you will invent it!

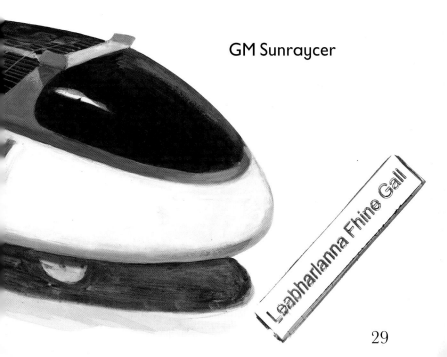

GM Sunraycer

Leabharlanna Fhine Gall

Glossary

 crankshaft A crankshaft is a metal rod. When the piston moves backwards and forwards, the crankshaft goes round and round. **16, 17**

 force Pushes and pulls are two kinds of force. **17**

 fumes When petrol burns, it gives off fumes. **25, 26, 27**

 gear A gear is a wheel with teeth. The teeth can fit into the teeth on another gear, and move it. **17, 22**

 invent When you think up a new machine or a new idea, you invent it. **8, 28, 29**

petrol Petrol is a clear liquid which burns very fast. **8, 16**

 piston A piston moves backwards and forwards in a tube called a cylinder when a car's engine is running. **16, 17**

 robot A robot is a machine. People programme it to do work for them. **10**

 smog Smog is a mixture of smoke and fog in the air. **26**

 spark plug When electricity goes through the spark plug, it makes a spark. **16**

Reading Together

Oxford Reds have been written by leading children's authors who have a passion for particular non-fiction subjects. So as well as up-to-date information, fascinating facts and stunning pictures, these books provide powerful writing which draws the reader into the text.

Oxford Reds are written in simple language, checked by educational advisors. There is plenty of repetition of words and phrases, and all technical words are explained. They are an ideal vehicle for helping your child develop a love of reading – by building fluency, confidence and enjoyment.

You can help your child by reading the first few pages out loud, then encourage him or her to continue alone. You could share the reading by taking turns to read a page or two. Or you could read the whole book aloud, so your child knows it well before tackling it alone.

Oxford Reds will help your child develop a love of reading and a lasting curiosity about the world we live in.

Sue Palmer
Writer and Literacy Consultant